THE WHIMSICAL LIFE OF MAX THE DOG

Makes Pancakes

Allen R. McCaulley

Visit us at WhimsicalMax.com

Copyright © 2021 by Allen R. McCaulley

Jacket and interior illustrations by Tatiana (Tanya) Panova

Edited by Louanne Piccolo

All rights reserved. No part of this book may be reproduced or used in any manner without the prior written permission of the copyright owner, except as permitted by United States copyright law. To request permissions, please contact us at whimsicalmax@outlook.com, or Allen R. McCaulley, P.O. Box 1613, Moline, IL 61265

ISBN: 9781736627600 (hardcover); ISBN: 9781736627617 (paperback)
LCCN: 2021913196 (hardcover); LCCN: 2021914056 (paperback)

Thank you to my wife, Linnea—your interest and support of this story was tremendously helpful.

Thank you to Lou—this project wouldn't have happened without your help and kindness.

Thank you to Tanya—your talent is on every page; your goodwill made this project a joy.

Thank you to Gwen for putting the puzzle pieces together and making them into a book.

And Max, our buddy. Your Mom and I miss you. You are forever in our hearts. We love you.

"Max, Mom has to go to the grocery store and then over to see your Grandma. You be a good dog until I get back."

Max hopped off the couch and headed out to the kitchen. He was home alone, and he could do whatever he wanted to do.

There it was, right in front of him. He loved the smells that came from the refrigerator.

But how could he open the door?

He looked around, and looked again. And then Max had an idea.

There was a dishtowel hanging from the refrigerator door handle. That was never there, but it was today.

So, he pulled on the towel.

But the door did not open.

He tried again, and pulled harder. A lot harder. So hard that the dishtowel fell to the floor. Then...

Bang! Crash! Thud!

A carton of eggs, a tub of butter, a bag of flour, and a carton of milk all landed on the floor.

Two of the eggs rolled out of the carton and across the floor.

A half-eaten hot dog hit Max on the head.

Chomp! Chomp! Chomp!

Max devoured the hot dog and licked his lips.

That was easy.

But what to do with the eggs, and butter, and flour, and milk?

And then Max had an idea.

He was a smart dog, and he knew what to do. Max was going to make pancakes. He had watched his Mom do it, and he knew he could too.

Max needed a bowl to make pancakes. He swatted one from the table.

BOOM!

Thank goodness it didn't break," thought Max.

SPLAT! SPLAT!
went two eggs into the mixing bowl, shells and all.

Then, Max dumped some of the flour into the bowl.

KERPLUNK!
went the butter.

Next came the milk.

Max needed to stir the milk into the mixture, but he didn't know what to use to stir it.

And then Max had an idea.

His right paw might work.

So, he stirred and stirred some more.

It Worked!

He didn't even spill any on the carpet.

Max dragged a hot plate out from the cupboard,
plugged it in
and the first pancake was done in a jiffy,
and then another.

All of a sudden Max sat up straight.

He listened very intently.

Max heard sounds from miles away. And, he recognized that sound. Oh no! It was his Mom's car. At least it was still a couple of miles away.

Max had a problem.

He had to put everything back very quickly, but he had closed the refrigerator door earlier and couldn't open it again.

What to do?

And then Max had an idea.

Max hid the bowl of pancake mix behind a log in the fireplace.

That was easy.

The sound of the car was closer.

There was still time, but Max had to hurry.

The flour was next.

There was a potted plant in the dining room,
and Max put the flour inside it.

The car was getting closer, and closer, but Max still had time.

What to do with the carton of eggs?

Max looked and looked and listened
as the sound of the car got closer.

"I know! Behind the living room
couch is the best place," he thought.

What about the tub of butter?

Max looked and looked and finally put it behind the television in the living room.

Max was sure that he had taken care of everything.
After all, he was a smart dog.

But there was one thing Max had missed.

While he was hiding the tub of butter behind the television,
someone was looking through the living room window.

And, what do you think she saw?

CPSIA information can be obtained
at www.ICGtesting.com
Printed in the USA
BVHW051715251021
619840BV00002B/41